Going to the Movies

Julie Haydon

Contents

Chapter 1 — Saturday

I am staying at Uncle Brett's for the weekend.

Today Uncle Brett took me to see a movie.

First, we looked on the **Internet** to see what movies were on.

3

Uncle Brett wanted to go
to the **local** cinema centre.
A lot of movies for children were on.
I picked one for us to see.

Chapter 2

The Cinema Centre

We went to the cinema centre.
We had to line up to buy our tickets.

Uncle Brett let me buy some popcorn and a drink from the candy bar.

THE CAT IN THE HAT

There were lots of movie posters
at the cinema centre.
I liked looking at them.

Chapter 3

Cinema Nine

I gave our tickets to an **usher**.
He checked the tickets,
then he tore them in half.
He gave us back our ticket **stubs**.

Peter
Pan

There were ten cinemas at the centre.
Our movie was showing in cinema nine.

The lights were on in the cinema.
It was full of rows of seats.
There was a huge **screen**
at the front of the cinema.

Uncle Brett and I sat down in our seats.
Other people came in and sat down too.

Then the lights slowly went off
and music started playing.
Uncle Brett and I watched the screen.

Chapter 4

On the Big Screen

It was dark in the cinema now.
Advertisements started playing
on the screen.

Then the movie began.
It was loud and full of colour.
The pictures on the screen moved quickly.
It was so exciting!

Names came up on the screen.
They were some of the people
who had made the movie.
The name of the movie
came up on the screen too.

PETER PAN

Sometimes it was funny.
Sometimes it was exciting.
Sometimes it was a little sad.
I was having great fun!

The movie ended ninety minutes later.
We left the cinema and talked about the movie.

I thanked Uncle Brett for taking me
to the movies.
Then I asked him how movies are made.
What a day!

Chapter 5

Making a Movie

A writer writes the story, or **screenplay**.
The screenplay has all the words
that the actors will say in the movie.

Green light from the spacecraft streams in through the
Danny wakes and sits up in fright.

DANNY
(loud
Dad! It's

Danny runs
Suddenly the
Enter Dad.

ashing lights.
is left in darkn

DAD
Danny. It's th

DANNY
But Dad, they

Screenplay

DAD
Go back to sleep,

enough of this nonsens

The person who tells everyone what to do while the movie is being made is the **director**.

Peter Jackson was the director of *The Lord of the Rings* movies.

Actors play the people in movies.
Some actors are very famous.

Naomi Watts

Orlando Bloom

Movies are made on film.
Lots of film is used.
A film **editor** puts the best bits
of film together to make the movie.

Lots of other people work on a movie too.

There are people who:

* ✳ work the cameras
* ✳ work the lights
* ✳ make the **sets**

* get the sound right
* work on computers
* find or make clothes for the actors
* put make-up on the actors.

Glossary

advertisements	messages that tell people about things they can buy
director	a person who is the boss while a movie is being made
editor	a person who puts bits of film together to make a movie
Internet	lots of computers that are linked together and share information
local	not far away
screen	a blank area in a cinema that you look at to watch a movie
screenplay	a written story for a movie
sets	furniture, buildings and other things that are made for movies
stubs	left-over parts of tickets
usher	a person who works in a cinema or theatre taking tickets and showing people to their seats

Index